DYLAN'S AMAZING DINOSAURS

THE STEGOSAURUS

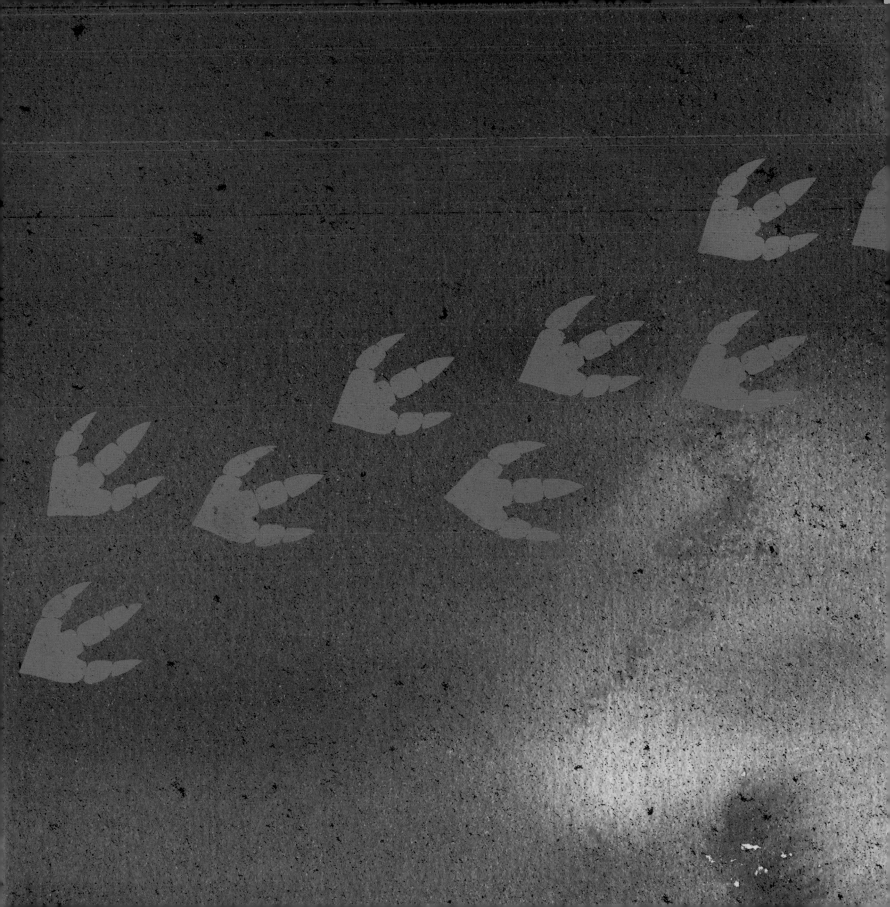

To Tamara, for your wonderful friendship
and extraordinary imagination x – E.H.

For Sam – D.T.

SIMON AND SCHUSTER
First published in Great Britain in 2014 by Simon and Schuster UK Ltd • 1st Floor, 222 Gray's Inn Road, London WC1X 8HB • A CBS Company • Text copyright © 2014 E.T. Harper • Illustrations copyright © 2014 Dan Taylor
Paper engineering by Maggie Bateson • Concept © 2014 Simon and Schuster UK • The right of E. T. Harper and Dan Taylor to be identified as the author and illustrator of this work has been asserted by them
in accordance with the Copyright, Designs and Patents Act, 1988. • All rights reserved, including the right of reproduction in whole or in part in any form • A CIP catalogue record for this book
is available from the British Library upon request • ISBN: 978 1 4711 1936 1 • eBook ISBN: 978 1 4711 1937 8 • Printed in China • 10 9 8 7 6 5 4 3 2 1

DYLAN'S AMAZING DINOSAURS

THE STEGOSAURUS

E.T. HARPER AND DAN TAYLOR

SIMON AND SCHUSTER

London   New York   Sydney   Toronto   New Delhi

Dylan's tree house was incredible. It was full of extraordinary things, and the most extraordinary of all were Grandpa Fossil's magic Dinosaur Journal and . . .

Keep Out!

WINGS, his toy pterodactyl!

'I wonder what amazing dinosaur discovery we'll make today?' Dylan said as he flung open the journal.

Fact File
Name: Stegosaurus —
or 'Roofed Lizard'
Diet: Plants
Habitat: North America
and Asia
Unusual features: Triangular
plates running from neck to
tail. Really small brain . . .
the size of a walnut!
Secret Weapon: Thagomizer

Stegosaurus

Thagomizer
?

Plates

'I think we've found our Dino Mission — to find out
what a thagomizer is! Let's go Wings!' said Dylan excitedly.

As soon as he heard the magic words Wings came
to life and flew off the shelf.

'Let's go, let's soar . . . off to the land
where the dinosaurs roar!' Dylan shouted as they
took off from the tree house deck.

'Look there's a group of stegs!

Hmm . . . I wonder what a thagomizer could possibly look like,' Dylan thought aloud as they flew over Roar Island. 'Could it be like a sword? Or a spike?

WOOOOAAAHHHH!' he cried as Wings swooped over a cliff.

Dylan spotted a lone dinosaur
running as fast as it could along the bank of a river.

'Look at that stegosaurus, Wings!' Dylan exclaimed.

'Wowsers it's moving fast!'
Dylan soon saw why – just behind it was
an allosaurus in hot pursuit.

But the poor stegosaurus was running out
of steam and slowing down . . .

'Uh-oh!' Dylan shouted. 'It's been separated from the others!
Look, they're on the other side of the river.
If it can just make it to them it will be safe.

Over there!' he called, jumping and pointing.
'Your herd is just there –

AAARRRGGGHHHH!'

The cliff had crumbled beneath him and Dylan was sliding straight towards the dinosaurs!

Dylan landed safely on top of the rocks that had crumbled down from the cliff.

'Phew, that was close!' said Dylan. 'But look, all these rocks have blocked the allosaurus. It can't reach the stegosaurus now!'

But Dylan had spoken a little too soon.
Before the steg could escape, the allosaurus
jumped on top of the rocks and roared.

The stegosaurus stopped to face the allosaurus.
'Oh no, Wings, the only thing that can save it now
are those super-strong plates!' said Dylan.

Sure enough the stegosaurus turned to bare its plates towards the approaching allosaurus and the fight began. THWAAACCCKKKK!

'It may lack brains but it's definitely brave!' said Dylan as the stegosaurus thumped the allosaurus in the jaw.

THWUUUUUMMMMMPPP!

The allosaurus was strong though and floored the stegosaurus in one go.

'Come on, Steg!' shouted Dylan. 'Get up!'

Just when they thought it was all over, the stegosaurus used its last bit of energy to whip up its mighty tail and . . .

BANG!

'Wow!' Dylan exclaimed. 'Look at those spikes, they're an awesome secret weapon. Hang on! That's it! They're the THAGOMIZER!'

The allosaurus was knocked out. Wings hopped over the fallen dinosaur as Dylan saw his chance to help the stegosaurus get back to its herd.

'Quick Wings, I have a plan!' he said as he climbed on to the pterodactyl.

He reached into his rucksack and pulled out his packed lunch.
'Fly close to the stegosaurus, Wings!'

They swooped down and Dylan bravely put out his hand
to let the huge creature sniff the carrot he was holding.

'That's it, Steg! Come on!'
They flew over a fallen tree dropping
a trail of carrots along it.
The stegosaurus crunched them one by one
and crossed to the safety of its herd.

'Time to go home, I think,' said Dylan.

As the pair flew over the cliff top the allosaurus's eyes opened –
it had spotted them!

'Higher, Wings!' Dylan yelled.

They soared upwards just as the
dino's jaws snapped beneath them.

'Dino Mission accomplished!' Dylan shouted triumphantly
as they launched themselves head first back into the tree house.

LUNCH

'That stegosaurus's secret weapon is pretty cool,' he said,
sketching the picture of the thagomizer into the Dinosaur Journal.

As he closed the journal he turned to say goodbye to his faithful flying friend.

'You're my secret weapon, Wings!' Dylan smiled and crunched the last carrot.

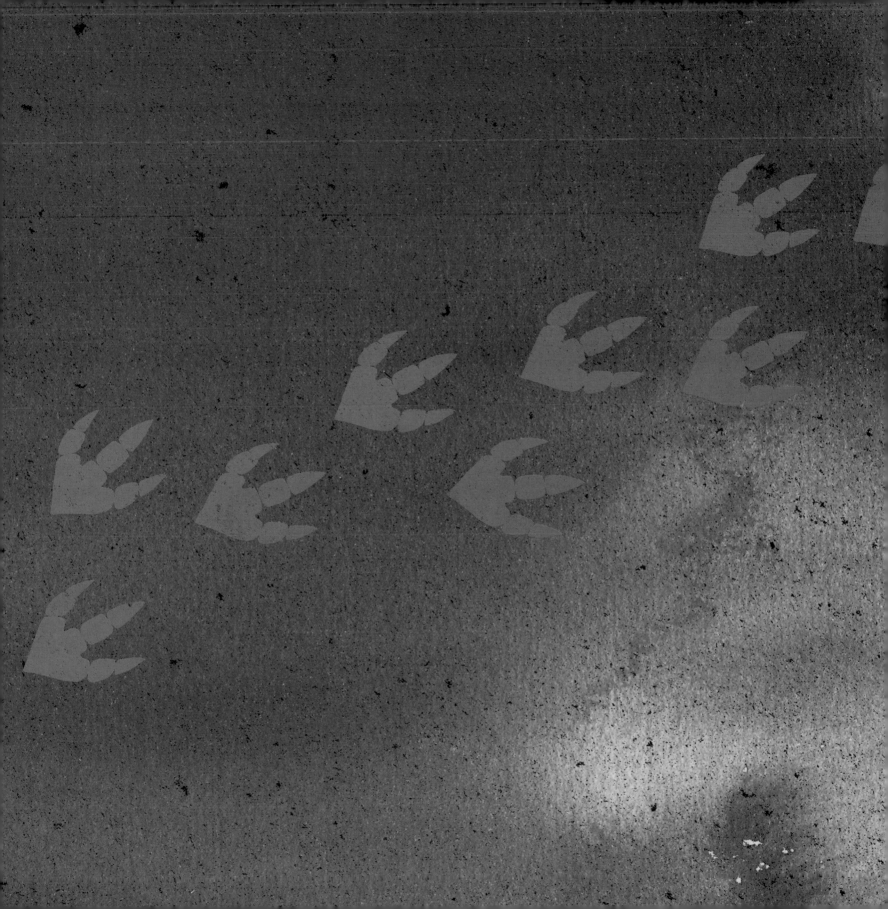

Look out for more amazing adventures
with Dylan and Wings!

Out now -
The Tyrannosaurus Rex

Coming soon -
The Spinosaurus
The Triceratops